I Am America

LINES WE DRAW

◆

A Story of Imprisoned Japanese Americans

Book design by Jake Slavik
Illustrations by Eric Freeberg

Photographs ©: National Archives Catalog, 150 (top), 150 (bottom), 151 (top), 151 (bottom); North Star Editions, 153

Published in the United States by Jolly Fish Press, an imprint of North Star Editions, Inc.

First Edition
First Printing, 2018

This is a work of fiction. Names, characters, places, and incidents are either the product of the author's imagination or are used fictitiously, and any resemblance to actual persons living or dead, business establishments, events, or locales is entirely coincidental.

Library of Congress Cataloging-in-Publication Data
Names: Lee, Camellia (Children's author), author. | Freeberg, Eric,
  illustrator.
Title: Lines we draw : a story of imprisoned Japanese Americans / by Camellia
  Lee ; illustrated by Eric Freeberg.
Description: Mendota Heights, MN : Jolly Fish Press, [2019] | Series: I am
  America | Summary: "Sumiko Adachi's life is uprooted when an arbitrary
  dividing line through Phoenix forces her family into a confinement camp"—
  Provided by publisher.
Identifiers: LCCN 2018038113 (print) | LCCN 2018041144 (ebook) | ISBN
  9781631632815 (e-book) | ISBN 9781631632808 (pbk.) | ISBN 9781631632792
  (hardcover)
Subjects: LCSH: Japanese Americans—Evacuation and relocation,
  1942-1945—Juvenile fiction. | CYAC: Japanese Americans—Evacuation and
  relocation, 1942-1945—Fiction. | Poston Relocation Center
  (Ariz.) —Fiction. | World War, 1939-1945—United States—Fiction. | Family
  life—Arizona—Fiction. | Arizona—History—1912-1950—Fiction. | LCGFT:
  Fiction.
Classification: LCC PZ7.L394867 (ebook) | LCC PZ7.L394867 Li 2019 (print)
LC record available at https://lccn.loc.gov/2018038113

Jolly Fish Press
North Star Editions, Inc.
2297 Waters Drive
Mendota Heights, MN 55120
www.jollyfishpress.com

Printed in the United States of America

I Am America

LINES WE DRAW

◆

A Story of Imprisoned Japanese Americans

By Camellia Lee

Illustrated by Eric Freeberg

Consultant: Stephen Vlastos, Professor Emeritus,
Department of History, University of Iowa

JOLLY
FiSH
PRESS

Mendota Heights, Minnesota

Terms

Issei – first-generation Japanese immigrants living in America. These people were ineligible for citizenship until the law changed in 1952.

Nisei – second-generation Japanese Americans, born in the United States and US citizens. The bulk of those forced into prison camps were of this generation.

Obaasan – Grandma in Japanese

Ojiisan – Grandpa in Japanese

Relocation center – the official government term for the ten prison camps to which Japanese Americans living in western states were forcibly relocated; the centers were run by the War Relocation Authority.

PROLOGUE

The Dream

In my dream, I stood barefoot in a mossy forest. The clouds covered the moon, and all at once I knew I wasn't alone. There was something just behind me. I heard it snarl. It was a wolf. I tried to run—no, float—away, but I wasn't moving. I didn't know where Mama or Papa were; they were there, but then they weren't. It was like *Little Red Riding Hood* come to life.

Where was I? The forest loomed around me, and there was a mass of dark shapes (were they people?) that watched me. Then suddenly there were more wolves around me. Their faces were peaceful, but they joined the chase. I wanted to stop but couldn't. I had to keep running.

I ran down paths. I jumped over rocks and stumps. I could feel the wolves' teeth nipping at my heels, just out of reach. I kept thinking that any minute one would catch me, but they never seemed able to keep up. Still, there were always more wolves lurking ahead of me. I could feel their breath.

The wolves seemed to be both losing and gaining on me.

I yelled, "Go ahead of me! I'm not here!"

They laughed like humans and kept running, the forest moving them along.

Suddenly, a cliff loomed in front of me; its craggy, sharp rocks broke the ocean far below. My body bent, and I jumped.

I landed in the desert. I was looking at the farmers working our fields. The wolves and dark, misty greenery had vanished.

PART I

At Home in Phoenix

Chapter One

Sumiko Adachi's legs kicked violently, twisting the sheets until they became tightly bound around her ankles.

She woke.

Her heart was pounding. Her damp fists were clenched tight. Her face was wet with tears.

For several minutes she couldn't believe it was only a nightmare. It had all seemed so real. She could almost taste the air as it hit her face while she ran from the wolves.

Sumiko shuddered and blinked hard, trying to see where she was. She gathered herself into a small ball and hugged her knees. Gradually, her heart rate slowed, and she could see that she was safe in her room in Phoenix. She took a deep breath and wiped her face with her hand. Shaking too much to get out of bed, she stared into the darkness. Traces of early-morning light were just beginning to emerge. Finally, she could make out familiar things in her room: the big carved-oak chest of drawers that her father had built, the small velvet armchair that was her favorite place to be in the whole house, and the large framed watercolor with scenes of a day at the beach.

Yes, everything was there. It was all right. She was safe and didn't need to escape a pack of hungry wolves.

In fact, she remembered, *it's the first day of school.*

She took a deep breath and got out of bed. Her stomach turned as she got dressed for the new day. Walking toward the kitchen, she tried to put the dream behind her.

The kitchen smelled faintly of the chicken and noodles from last night's dinner. *If only I hadn't eaten the last piece for supper so that I could have some for lunch.* She stared into the cold, organized-to-perfection refrigerator and contemplated her bagged lunch. She had first-day-of-school jitters, and food was always her comfort.

Sumiko's mother came into the kitchen, her bathrobe trailing behind her like a cape. As Sumiko buttered some bread, her mama poured her a glass of milk. Sitting down for breakfast with her mother, the despair of the nightmare slowly melted away. Unfortunately, Sumiko's attention turned to another fear: Today was her first day in a new school.

Sumiko smoothed her shoulder-length, dark hair and looked around her classroom at Phoenix Elementary. She already felt like an outsider. It seemed like everyone knew everyone else. The other students already had friends. Sumiko's light-brown eyes studied the school's students, so different from the segregated school she attended last year.

She hoped that the other students would be friendly. Sumiko knew that some people in America didn't like her and her family because of their Japanese heritage. And it wasn't just because there was a war going on and—although the United States remained neutral—tensions with Japan were rising. The anti-Japanese sentiment had been simmering for as long as she could remember. Once, a car dealer refused to let her father buy a car. When Sumiko was out with her family, she sometimes felt the eyes of strangers boring into her. Sumiko's stomach turned whenever she thought about the treatment her family received.

Sitting in front of Sumiko was the only other Japanese American student in the class. The girl looked familiar. She had soft, dark hair cut short behind her ears, pale skin, and bright hazel-green eyes. Her hands were folded as she listened attentively to Mrs. Fields, their teacher, give directions for the morning. The girl looked like the model student, but her bright-pink dress and yellow Mary Janes demanded attention. Sumiko had never seen yellow Mary Janes before and wondered if the girl had painted them herself.

Mrs. Fields wrote "My Summer Memories" on the chalkboard and then walked to her desk to get worksheets for the class. As soon as Mrs. Fields turned her back, the girl turned around and whispered to Sumiko, "Hi, I'm Emi."

Sumiko smiled back. "Hi, I'm Suzie. Your family owns Kuno's Market in town, right?" She glanced over at Mrs. Fields.

"Yeah," Emi said, not even lowering her voice. "I remember seeing you come by with your family. Do you still shop—?"

"Quiet down, please," said Mrs. Fields as she passed out the worksheets.

Sumiko ducked her head and looked down at her worksheet. She began writing about her summer memories.

Another classmate, pudgy-cheeked Jimmy, reached over and stole the eraser from Sumiko's desk when he thought no one was looking. He snickered. Mrs. Fields looked up from her desk and squinted at the class through her thick, round glasses.

"Be respectful, friends," Mrs. Fields said to no one in particular.

Jimmy made faces at Mrs. Fields when she looked back down at whatever she was reading. Emi glared at Jimmy and snatched the eraser back. She handed it back to Sumiko.

"Thanks," Sumiko whispered to Emi. Sumiko had a hard time containing her smile. She had a friend.

August 18, 1941
Dear Diary,

I met a new girl in class today. Her name is Emi Kuno. Well, actually, I've met her before. Her family owns the grocery store Kuno's Market. When I was younger, we used to shop there. It was before another grocery store opened closer to our farm. We would sell our lettuce and cantaloupe to Kuno's and then buy other things we needed. Kuno's is always busy. People go there to buy Japanese foods that they can't get anywhere else. The Kuno family also lives there, I think, in a basement home under the store.

Kuno's Market used to be my favorite place to go with Papa. Mr. Kuno always gave me candy out of a large jar on the counter after he selected the fruits and vegetables that he wanted to sell. That's when I first met Emi.

Emi would practice her dance steps on the counter where we paid! She was really good too. I asked her how she knew how to dance like that and she said, "Just practice." It's so neat to be going to school with her now. I hope we'll be friends.

Sumiko

US ENACTS OIL EMBARGO IN RESPONSE TO JAPANESE AGGRESSION IN PACIFIC

Due to increasing Japanese aggression in the Pacific, tensions between the United States and Japan have never been higher. Japan's increasing occupation of Southeast Asia has resulted in US sanctions that have the two nations on the brink of war.

The latest sanction, which took effect August 1, will halt US oil shipments to Japan. This is expected to be a huge blow to the Japanese war effort, as Japan gets 80 percent of its oil from the United States. The oil embargo follows soon after the freezing of all Japanese assets in America that took effect July 26.

These sanctions are designed to put pressure on Japan to withdraw from the territories it holds in Indochina. The Japanese occupation is a threat to American forces stationed in the nearby Philippines.

President Roosevelt has so far been reluctant to involve the United States in the growing global conflict. But unless Japanese-American relations can be mended soon, war could be an inevitability.

Chapter Two

"Would you like to come over to my house this weekend, Suzie?" Emi asked. It was the end of the first week of school and all around them kids were hurrying to leave. Today Emi's dress was a bright blue, and she had matching barrettes pulling her hair back just behind her ears.

"That would be fun," Sumiko said. She'd always wanted to see Emi's home. When she visited Kuno's Market, she had always tried to imagine what the living area looked like downstairs.

"Great, it'll be just you and me. What about Saturday at six o'clock?" Emi asked. When Sumiko agreed, Emi practically danced. Then she squeezed Sumiko's arms and got in line for the crowded farm truck taking her to Mesa. "See you then!" she trilled.

August 22, 1941
Dear Diary,

The first week of school was tough and I'm really tired. There's a lot of history and math that I need to study. My spelling is really bad, especially for the longer words. I've been making up songs to help myself remember all the letters in each word.

Luckily, tomorrow is Saturday and I can sleep in—or so Mama says. She's been distracted lately, so I guess she's not going to make me do my usual Saturday chores! HOORAY! Of course, I can't sleep too late. Emi Kuno invited me to come to her house. When school started at the beginning of the week, I thought I was going to spend the whole year with no friends. I'm so glad that Emi wants to be friends.

Emi isn't anything like me. She likes

to stand out with her colorful outfits and upbeat personality. She seems to know what's going on with every kid in our school. While I'd be content to hide in the corner, she likes to be the center of attention.

Even though we're very different, I think she will make a great friend.

Sumiko

Chapter Three

September 4, 1941
Dear Diary,

Studying, studying, studying! I have been studying so much lately that I don't have much time for anything else, including seeing Emi. We had fun at her house on Saturday. Her dad even remembered how much I liked the candy jar, and he offered me candy when I arrived. I'm a lot older than I was when my family used to visit the store, but I still like candy!

Emi invited me to her house after school again yesterday, but I said I couldn't go. We had a history test today, and I knew Mama would be unhappy if I didn't study all afternoon and evening for it. I think I did pretty well on it. I hope so after all that studying!

Mama's always telling me how important my education is. My parents came to Arizona in search

of a better life for our family and for my future.
The way Mama tells the story, Papa came home one
day with a look of determination on his face.

"We're leaving California, Haruko," he said to my
mama.

"I guess he saw one too many 'Japs Keep Moving'
signs," Mama always says.

But the land in Glendale was plentiful and cheap,
and my parents were able to get a twenty-acre
parcel. It's a nice piece of land, with a low creek
running through the middle. We lease the land from
the Millers.

"It was hard work to get the land flowing with
fruit and vegetables," Papa likes to remind me.

I see the hard work they put in. The land is
hot and the days are long for farmers like us.
And that's why I keep up with my schoolwork. My
parents work hard for me to get an education, so I
will work hard too. It's the least I can do.

Sumiko

September 12, 1941
Dear Diary,

We're on our way to Los Angeles to visit my grandparents for the weekend. I can't wait to see them—and California! Emi is jealous because she thinks I'm going to see movie stars in Hollywood like Cary Grant and Rosalind Russell. But I'm just excited to see my grandparents!

My family moved to Arizona from California when I was three years old. I haven't seen Obaasan and Ojiisan since I was four years old, and I don't remember living in California. I don't even remember what it is like.

Maybe I should color my hair to look like a movie star. On second thought, I don't think I'd like that. Everyone would stare at me. But it's definitely something that Emi would try!

Sumiko

September 15, 1941
Dear Diary,

Los Angeles was so much fun. I like my grandparents' house with its orange trees.

On Saturday, we drove to the mountains and had a picnic. Obaasan brought along some great food: apple pie, watermelon, karaage, and korokke. It was delicious. It was so good that a clever little squirrel came up to get the crumbs off our blanket. Obaasan laughed at that.

In the mountains, the air felt like autumn. It was so much cooler than Arizona! And the trees were lovely: yellow, red, and gold. I don't ever stop to notice the beauty of nature in Arizona. Maybe it's because I am always so busy! We have a very long summer in Arizona—almost an <u>eternal</u> heat. That's a word that Mrs. Fields would like.

When I got to school today, Emi wanted to know what movie stars I had seen. Unfortunately, I had to disappoint her because I didn't see any. Maybe next time!

Sumiko

"That film was swell," Emi said. Her eyes had a far-off, dreamy look to them.

"It really was neat," Sumiko agreed.

The girls met after school to see a movie and then went to a nearby a restaurant. Sumiko took a deep breath. The smells of spicy enchilada sauce, tortillas, and carne asada filled her nose. She looked around. The restaurant was an old pueblo with wooden beams on the ceiling and lots of chili peppers hanging on the walls.

It's so nice to be here with Emi, Sumiko thought. Neither girl had any siblings, and Sumiko felt like it was destiny that the two of them would become the best of friends.

Emi's voice shook Sumiko out of her daydreams. "I want to be a famous actress, I think. And then I could dance, just like Eleanor Powell."

"You'd be the first Japanese American movie star!" Sumiko said, taking a sip of her soda.

"You should be an actress too, Suzie. We could be a team," said Emi, her eyes glittering at the thought.

"Oh, thank you!" Sumiko blushed. "But I'm not sure about that. I'm not much of a dancer."

The girls were quiet for a moment.

"Did you always want to do that?" Sumiko asked. "Be an actress, I mean."

"Yes," Emi said. "Ever since I saw the first *Broadway Melody* film, I knew I was meant for the stage."

"Oh, that's nice." Sumiko wasn't sure what else to say. She spent so much time studying that she never really allowed herself to dream like Emi did.

Emi nodded her head in agreement. "It will be glamorous and exciting."

"Won't you be scared?" Sumiko asked.

Emi looked confused. "Scared of what?"

Sumiko shrugged. "Being in front of those people. Forgetting your lines or your dance steps."

Emi shook her head from side to side. "No. I wouldn't be scared. Not of that," she said.

Sumiko raised her eyebrows. "But you are scared of something, right?" Emi always seemed so fearless that

Sumiko was almost afraid to hear the answer to her question.

"Insects. I hate insects," said Emi, making a face.

Sumiko laughed. Growing up on a farm, Sumiko was used to insects. "Insects don't frighten me," she said. "But I am scared of wolves."

"Wolves?" Emi asked. "There aren't many wolves in Arizona, are there? Have you ever seen one before?"

Sumiko shook her head. "Well not exactly, but sometimes I have nightmares about them chasing me. No matter what I do, they keep coming after me."

Emi waved her hand dismissively. "But that's just a dream."

Sumiko shrugged her shoulders. "I guess."

Emi's face brightened. "Hey, you know what will cheer you up? I want to invite you to my birthday party! It's on October 11th."

"Oh, neat," Sumiko said. "I didn't know your birthday was coming up."

"Yup! It's not like a party you'd have for a little kid, though. No games or anything. I just want to see some of my best friends."

Sumiko shifted uneasily in her seat. She knew Emi had some friends in Mesa that went to a different school, but she wasn't sure that she wanted to meet them. Meeting new people always made her nervous.

Emi touched her friend's hand. "It will be a good time. I promise."

Sumiko smiled and nodded. "Okay, I'll ask my parents."

Emi grabbed Sumiko's arm. "It's getting late. We should probably head back home."

Chapter Four

October 10, 1941

WITH INCREASING THREAT OF WAR, ROOSEVELT SUPPORTS ROLLING BACK NEUTRALITY ACT

President Roosevelt called on Congress yesterday to relax portions of the Neutrality Act of 1939. The President specifically called for the repeal of Section Six, which prohibits civilian ships from carrying weapons. With German ships operating all over the world, it is becoming unsafe for American ships to be unprotected.

Indeed, German submarines have sunk numerous US ships in recent months. The attack prompted President Roosevelt last month to allow US Navy ships to fire at enemy ships on sight. The President does not want to be drawn into war but will not tolerate any further loss of American life.

The concerns about Section Six were just part of the President's address. He cautioned members of Congress about the quickly escalating conflict in Europe. If German Chancellor Adolf Hitler fully implements his military plans, then the United States is going to have to defend itself sooner or later.

$\mathcal{T}$he drive to Mesa for Emi's birthday party went faster than Sumiko anticipated. By the time her papa pulled up to Kuno's Market, her stomach was knotted with nerves.

What if no one talks to me? Sumiko took a breath, steeling herself for the event. After thanking Papa for the ride, she entered Kuno's Market and headed toward the back room. Emi's mother smiled when she saw Sumiko and led her down the stairs to the basement. Emi's Mesa friends, Lucy and Betty, were already there. Sumiko felt the girls' eyes on her.

The house was dark and a little musty smelling. But Emi had made it welcoming, with extra chairs and a table of food.

"Sumiko—I mean Suzie—these are my friends Lucy and Betty," Emi said.

"Hi," Sumiko said timidly.

Lucy was wearing a blue dress with sandals and had red curls cut above her ears. Betty had slightly longer blonde hair cut just below her chin.

"Suzie lives on a farm just outside of Phoenix," Emi said.

"Cheap labor," Betty said under her breath.

Sumiko's face flushed. *Is she talking about my family? Is she making fun of me?*

"I like the way you have your hair," Lucy said.

Instinctively, Sumiko's hand went up to the pink barrette holding her bangs back.

"I wish mine would grow already so that I could wear it in a ponytail," Lucy continued.

Sumiko didn't know how to respond to Betty's remark, so she didn't. To Lucy, she just said, "Um, thanks."

"How do you like Phoenix Elementary, Suzie?" Betty asked slowly, tilting her head to the side.

"It's better than my old school," Sumiko replied.

Betty kept staring at Sumiko, making her uncomfortable, while Lucy rattled on about the last history test at her school.

Sumiko was pretty sure that she didn't like Betty. She looked to the food table next to her and spotted a bowl of candy, dug for a chocolate, opened it, and took a small bite.

Although she wasn't hungry, she was anxious and needed something to do.

The steps upstairs beckoned, and Sumiko excused herself to use the bathroom. But she really just stared in the mirror. *Why is Emi friends with a girl like Betty?* This party was worse than Sumiko could've imagined.

As she walked back down the stairs, she heard whispered and rushed voices coming from the girls below. Sumiko stopped short before the girls could see she was there.

"What's wrong with you two? I really like her," Emi said defensively.

"Have you ever been to her house before? On the farm?" The voice was Betty's.

"Sure. I don't go there often, though," Emi said. But she was lying. Emi hadn't been to Sumiko's house yet.

"Don't you think people out there are a little strange?" Betty asked. Her voice was dripping with superiority.

"I'm not sure what you mean," Emi responded slowly. "I guess I wasn't there for long. Suzie's papa doesn't like too many people coming over."

"Yeah, well, some people don't like Orientals taking over," Betty said.

Sumiko gasped. *Betty was awful.* She waited for Emi's fiery temper to take over, for her to call Betty out on the horrible things she was saying.

But Emi was silent.

"And did you say her name was *Sumiko?*" Betty continued. "What kind of name is that?" She laughed.

Sumiko couldn't stand to hear any more. She made a point to stomp down the last few steps and returned to the room. Her cheeks were burning, and she didn't care if the girls saw it.

"What did I miss?" Sumiko asked.

"N-Nothing," Emi stammered. "Suzie, help me get the popcorn?"

"Okay." Sumiko couldn't wait to get out of there. She followed Emi around the corner to the family's kitchen.

Once they were out of earshot, Emi said, "I'm sorry this isn't going well. I don't know what's got into Betty. She's not usually so . . . she's not usually like this."

Peals of laughter from the living room floated to their ears. Sumiko dreaded the rest of the evening: the pretending, the discomfort, the smirks that she'd pretend not to see. Tears began to well up in her eyes but she smiled a tight smile. It was Emi's birthday, after all.

"It's fine. I'm fine," Sumiko managed.

They carried bowls of popcorn back into the small living room. There was a tingling in the air that Sumiko could sense. It was like there was now an invisible line separating her and Emi from the other two girls.

The girls sat and the conversation was more relaxed as Lucy talked about a vacation she'd taken with her family over the summer, but Sumiko couldn't bring herself to join in with more than one-word answers.

"Is something wrong?" Lucy finally asked Sumiko.

Sumiko's head turned slightly toward Emi. *We're not Japanese American to them. Just Japanese. And they think of us as the enemy.* The words echoed over and over in her head, and she wondered if Emi could sense this too.

Chapter Five

November 27, 1941

US SECRETARY OF STATE HULL ISSUES DEMAND FOR JAPAN TO LEAVE INDOCHINA

After months of negotiations, the United States has made a written demand for Japan to withdraw from Indochina and China. The message was delivered to Japanese Ambassador Kichisaburo Nomura by US Secretary of State Cordell Hull. It contains a list of ten steps to be completed by the United States and Japan to ensure peace.

Proposals for a resolution have gone back and forth. Most recently, the United States rejected a proposal from the Japanese ambassador for a partial withdrawal from French Indochina in return for lifting of sanctions. The United States made very clear that they will not tolerate anything less than a full withdrawal of both Indochina and China. In exchange, the United States would unfreeze Japanese assets in America, the loss of which has crippled Japan. It remains to be seen whether that is enough motivation for Japan to give up its stronghold in Asia and avoid a larger war.

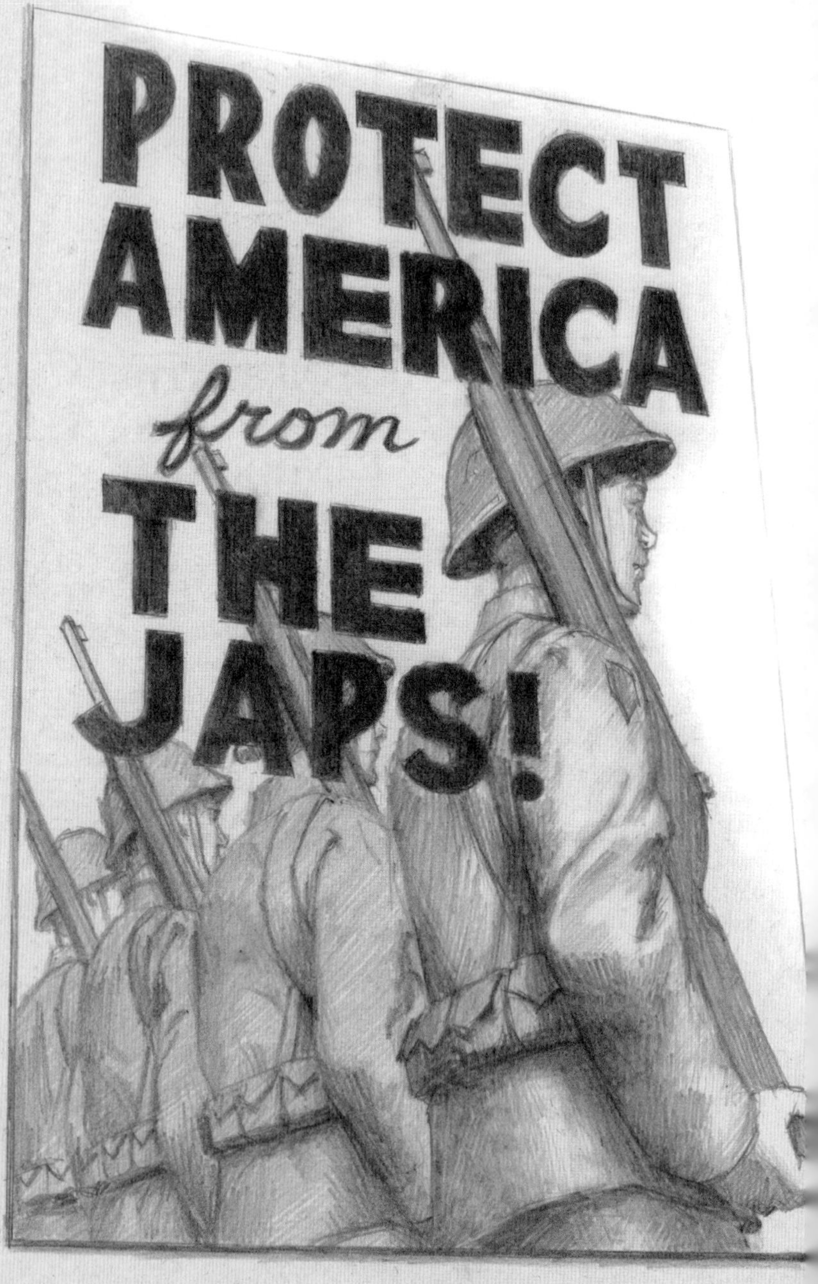
PROTECT AMERICA
from
THE JAPS!

Chapter Six

It was Monday morning, and Sumiko felt sick as she walked through the school doors. She'd heard about the attack on Pearl Harbor the day before. Her heart ached as she thought about the destruction and the deaths. She wondered if any of her classmates had family in Pearl Harbor.

As she hurried down the hallway to her classroom, she noticed the hushed voices and turned backs of students, leaving her a wide aisle to walk down. She caught a glance from Ruth, who sat to her left in class and was usually friendly. Ruth pretended not to see her and coldly turned around.

Sumiko looked for Emi in the hallway but couldn't find her in the mass of faces. She turned the corner and went into her classroom. Emi wasn't in her seat yet. Sumiko settled into her own chair.

Mrs. Fields started her lesson, and Sumiko watched as Emi quietly made her way in. She was late. Sumiko tried to catch her eye to mouth a hello, but Emi didn't look at her. Instead, Emi kept her head down.

Sumiko tried to concentrate on the lesson, but she couldn't help but feel like she was in some sort of dream. It was almost as if she were invisible. No one had spoken a word to her. Even Jimmy, who sat near her, didn't poke her to ask for a pencil or a piece of clean paper like he usually did. It was like Sumiko had done something wrong and the whole school knew about it.

What did I do?

Finally, at lunch, Sumiko got a chance to talk with Emi.

"Are you okay?" Sumiko asked. "Why were you late today?"

A cloud formed over Emi's face. "Some kids were being jerks to me. They threw my books in the bushes."

"What? Who?"

Emi shook her head. "I know I should tell Mrs. Fields, but I think that will make it worse. Japan bombed Pearl Harbor. You heard about that, right?"

"Yeah," Sumiko nodded. "Everyone knows."

"Don't you realize what might happen to us?" She had tears in her eyes now. Sumiko had never seen Emi so upset.

Sumiko put her arm around her friend.

"Not to us," Sumiko said. "We're Japanese *American*. We aren't the enemy."

A chill shot through Sumiko's body. She remembered Ruth turning away from her in the hall and her classmates casting sidelong glances her way all morning. *Maybe this is the start of bad things to come. Are people like Betty going to hate me even more now?*

Emi didn't look convinced. "Are you going to move or leave this school?" she asked.

"What?" Sumiko quickly pulled her arm off of her friend's shoulder as the gravity of the situation hit her. "Are you?"

Emi shrugged. She seemed so different from the confident, fun-loving girl that Sumiko knew her to be.

Sumiko looked around the cafeteria. She wondered if the other students really did think of her and Emi differently than before the attack. *I wonder if anyone is listening to us?* Sumiko wished there were an invisible wall she could put up around the two of them to protect them from their classmates.

Emi was inside her own private nightmare, too, and didn't seem to notice Sumiko's paranoia. "Some people don't want us here anymore," Emi said. "I overheard my parents talking about it yesterday."

Sumiko's face turned red and hot. She couldn't feel her feet. "What do you mean, they don't want us here? We're Americans."

"Well, we're Japanese too. The Japanese bombed us," Emi said.

"So what? That doesn't have anything to do with us," Sumiko said.

"Yes, but I'm not sure everyone feels that way. They think we're loyal to Japan."

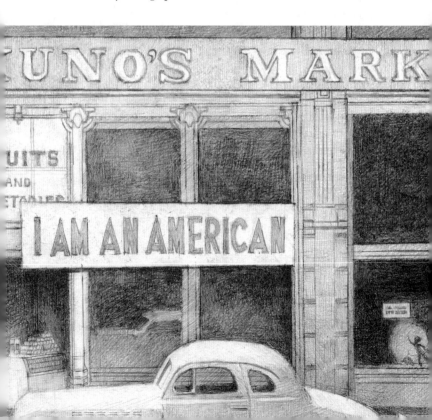

UNITED STATES DECLARES WAR ON JAPAN IN AFTERMATH OF PEARL HARBOR ATTACK

Calling December 7, the date of the Pearl Harbor attack, a "date which will live in infamy," President Franklin D. Roosevelt asked Congress to declare war on the Empire of Japan. That declaration was made within an hour of his address.

In his address, the President chided Japan for its false attempts at negotiating peace with the United States. Noting that such an attack must have been planned for some time, the President called out Japan's "false statements" and deliberate attempts to "deceive."

Hopes for peace were still alive as of late November, when it seemed like the two countries were working toward a negotiation. But Japan made its intentions clear with the sneak attack that has killed hundreds, if not thousands, of American soldiers. Japan has since also attacked numerous islands in the Pacific such as Guam and Midway.

With conflict ongoing in Europe, the world is truly at war.

Chapter Seven

December 10, 1941
Dear Diary,

The whole world has gone mad. It's as if overnight, the entire country hates me and people that look like me.

People have been calling the Japanese "Japs." That includes me and my family. They say things like, "You can't trust any of them" and, "Get them out of our state." In the lunchroom yesterday, someone called me and Emi "slanty-eyed Japs." I wanted to run to the bathroom and cry, but Emi said we should just ignore them. Still, it hurt.

The only kids I talk to in school now are Japanese—but that number is getting smaller as people leave school. I don't know where they are all going. For most of them, there have been no goodbyes.

I cannot understand why everyone hates my family now. We are American citizens. We're all on the same side!

Sumiko

December 11, 1941
Dear Diary,

Newspapers say that "Jap spies" stand ready to attack at any moment. The Issei, they say, bought land near airfields years ago in preparation for this war. They say Japanese farmers plow ditches in certain directions to signal to the Japanese enemy planes above.

Why don't people realize how ridiculous this all sounds? We're not spies. The only people I know that have even been to Japan are Obaasan and Ojiisan, and they haven't been there in over twenty years.

Papa says the newspapers are filled with lies. That Japan, Germany, and Italy are the enemies too. But then why are people acting like WE are the enemies?

Sumiko

$\mathcal{S}$umiko breathed a sigh of relief at the sound of Emi's voice.

"Are you okay?" Sumiko asked. She had called Emi on the telephone because Emi wasn't in school that day.

"Yes, yes, I'm fine," Emi said. "I'm just sick."

"Oh, that's too bad. But I'm relieved. I was worried you had left Mesa," Sumiko said.

"No, we're still here. I don't think my parents are planning to move, especially with the store and all," Emi said.

"I'm happy to hear that," Sumiko said. "I don't know what I'd do without you."

"I could say the same about you," Emi said. "I can tell my parents are really worried, though. I hear them whispering when they think I'm not around. Something's not right."

"It's the same thing at my house too."

The girls sat in silence for a moment until Sumiko asked, "Do you think we should be . . . afraid?"

"I don't know," Emi said. "I just don't know."

December 12, 1941
Dear Diary,

Something is coming.

    I'm supposed to be doing my homework right now, but I can't concentrate. I heard about my neighbors packing up and leaving, people who have lived here as long as I can remember.

    Papa tells me that we are Americans and that no one is out to get us. He says we need to carry on with the farm and things will get better. But if he's right, then why are so many people afraid? Why do I feel like I need to prove that I'm American?

    I feel like something bad is chasing us and I just can't get away.

                        Sumiko

Chapter Eight

December 16, 1941

NAVY SECRETARY FRANK KNOX BLAMES JAPANESE AMERICANS FOR PEARL HARBOR ATTACK

The question of how Japan pulled off its sneak attack on Pearl Harbor has no easy answer. But according to Secretary of the Navy Frank Knox, the blame rests with Japanese Americans. Knox returned from surveying the damage in Hawai'i with no doubt that "Japanese spies" were to blame.

In a press conference in Los Angeles, Knox warned of a "Fifth Column" of society. The Fifth Column would be a group of Japanese sympathizers working against the United States from within. Knox has been concerned about Japanese Americans for some time. As early as 1933, he argued for all people of Japanese descent to be confined in camps.

Knox will no doubt argue for confinement again after the attack on Pearl Harbor. Whether President Roosevelt would entertain such an extreme action remains to be seen.

December 16, 1941
Dear Diary,

All around us, people are leaving their homes to move somewhere else in the Valley or to other states, like Colorado, that are friendlier to Japanese Americans. I know Mama wants to do the same. I've heard her talking to Papa about it. But moving isn't an option for us, at least not right now. My parents have worked so hard to farm this land. If we went somewhere else, we'd have to start all over. But I think we are safe here. Nothing has happened to us . . . at least not yet.

Sumiko

December 19, 1941
Dear Diary,

Today in school, Jimmy told me that my family is taking his family's money away from him. Jimmy's family farms too. (Well, his mama does. His papa died a few years ago.) But it seems like there's plenty of work and money for everyone here.

It's horrible to say, but I'm getting used to the hateful looks and words that people say to me. I expect it to happen every day now. But that doesn't mean it doesn't hurt.

Sumiko

December 22, 1941
Dear Diary,

Christmas is coming soon, and I'm excited. With everything that has been happening, it's a relief to have something to look forward to. I have a record called Christmas Cheer that I've been playing over and over to get myself in the Christmas spirit.

At school today, I helped put up decorations in the gym. Our class is singing in the Christmas concert. Ruth asked me why I was there. She said, "Do you even celebrate Christmas?" I had to explain to her that yes, I am a Christian. That shut her up, which made me feel pretty good for standing up for myself.

I have been spending a lot of time with Emi, and Mama is teaching me to play the piano after school. I think I'm getting better. I don't mind when people listen as I play. I played a song for Emi last week and she danced along with it. Maybe Emi was right—we could be a Hollywood team someday.

Sumiko

December 25, 1941
Dear Diary,

It's Christmas! Even though we didn't have a tree this year (Mama said she just couldn't do it—maybe it's the war), our day was still perfect.

Like we've done for the past few years, we went to the Millers. Yes, even in the middle of a war, our German American neighbors (and friends!) had us over to celebrate. It was wonderful, with a big Christmas tree and a big Christmas dinner.

A surprise came too. Obaasan and Ojiisan called from California! It was so good to hear from them.

I hardly thought about the war the entire day. Surrounded by family, friends, and general Christmas cheer, it was easy not to.

I'm keeping my fingers crossed that the war will end soon. I wish every day were like this.

Sumiko

Chapter Nine

Sumiko knew something wasn't right as soon as she walked up the road to her house.

There was a strange car parked in front, and she couldn't see her mama or papa working in the fields. *It's too early to have stopped work for the day.* Sumiko readjusted her schoolbag on her shoulder and reached out a trembling hand to open the screen door to her house.

Her mama was sitting on the couch, her hands in her lap and her back stick-straight. Silently, Haruko motioned for her daughter to sit down beside her, and Sumiko did. Through the half-open door to the bedroom, Sumiko spied a white man with an overcoat rifling through her parents' belongings. He opened each drawer and dumped the contents onto the floor. Sumiko could tell her mother was trying to keep her composure.

The white man checked their closets. It seemed like he

had opened everything already, but he continued. Sumiko

wasn't sure what he was searching for.

"Where is Papa?" Sumiko asked her mother in her

softest voice. "Did they arrest him?"

Mama shook her head. "He's irrigating," she whispered, glancing out the window.

Don't come inside, Sumiko screamed in her mind.

The agents—there were two of them, Sumiko realized—were absorbed in their work. An agent with a fedora had just moved to search Sumiko's bedroom too. She saw him looking at drawings in her sketchbook. Angry, frustrated, and humiliated, Sumiko squirmed in her seat while the man scoured the rest of her room.

The agents consulted one another in low voices. Finally, after what seemed like an eternity, they walked to where Sumiko and her mama were seated in the living room.

"This is a nice Christian family," one of them said, with a hint of condescension in his voice. Neither agent stopped walking, however. They both continued for the door.

When the agents finally exited the house, Sumiko and Mama collapsed in their seats. They hugged one another without saying a word. *What would we have done if they had seen something that made us seem like spies?*

Sumiko and Mama scrambled to clean up their home.

February 19, 1942

ROOSEVELT SIGNS
EXECUTIVE ORDER 9066

President Roosevelt issued Executive Order 9066 that gives the Army authority to establish military zones anywhere in the United States from which any person, citizen or alien, may be evacuated and excluded.

The order is expected to go into effect in California and the Pacific Coast states as rapidly as conditions permit. No other geographical sections of the country are at present included.

Those chiefly affected are American citizens of Japanese parentage. Approximately 60,000 of those reside in California and an additional 14,000 are scattered throughout Oregon and Washington.

Lieutenant General John L. DeWitt, commanding general for the Western Defense Command, will have full discretion both as to the areas to be designated and the persons to be evacuated.

-NOTICE!-
TO ALL JAPANESE PERSONS AND PERSONS OF JAPANESE RACIAL ORIGIN

Take note that no persons of Japanese racial origin can be outside their homes between the hours of 8:00 p.m. and 6:00 a.m. Any persons who are found to have violated this order will face penalties.

JAPANESE AMERICANS
GIVEN SIX DAYS TO LEAVE HOMES

Japanese Americans in portions of Alameda County, California, have less than one week to move. That's the instruction given to all people of Japanese ancestry in Civilian Exclusion Order No. 34.

Before 12:00 p.m. on May 9, all people of Japanese ancestry must report to a Civil Control Station for transfer to an Assembly Center. From there, they will be moved more permanently to a Relocation Center. One such center is open so far: the Manzanar War Relocation Center near Independence, Calif. More are expected to open.

The focus of the evacuation is Military Area No. 1, established in March. Evacuation orders began later that month. So far, evacuations have been limited to people near military bases, "enemy aliens," and others. But this latest order will affect up to 120,000 people.

Approximately 1,000 Japanese Americans are arriving per day at Manzanar, but expect that number to climb.

Chapter Ten

May 30, 1942

MAIN STREET DIVIDES ARIZONA TOWN IN TWO

As the War Relocation Authority works to round up the last of the Japanese Americans ordered to evacuate, one Arizona town has seen the division firsthand. Main Street in Mesa, Arizona, happens to be the dividing line for the military's exclusion area. That means that those living on one side of the street are safe, while the other side has to evacuate.

This division has separated families and friends based on where they live. But even those who are "safe" still face suspicion from other residents. And they are forbidden to cross into the exclusion area.

Many Japanese Americans can no longer shop or go other places they used to. Students have had to change schools. As a world war rages on, nobody knows when the relocated Japanese Americans will be allowed to return to their homes.

"Why would the president make all the Japanese leave if they weren't dangerous?" Jimmy asked.

Emi snorted but Sumiko sighed. She tried to keep to herself at school most days, especially since the announcement about the exclusion line, but her class was doing a research project and they were in the library gathering materials. This was unavoidable.

"My papa says there are a lot of reasons," Sumiko explained. "It's partly panic and partly because there are a lot of people who want to get rid of us."

Jimmy wasn't satisfied with that explanation. "Well, isn't it possible you might try to help Japan? Like my mama says, after all, they are your people."

"But it's not my country," protested Sumiko. "The United States is."

"Your own country taking you away from your home," he said reflectively.

"I'm just caught on the wrong side of the line," Sumiko said, feeling unimaginably hopeless and lost. She'd found out last night that her family lived in the exclusion area. They were going to have to leave their home.

Sumiko caught Emi's eye. The look held a mixture of pain, anger, sadness, and relief. Emi's family would not be incarcerated. They were on the other side of the line. The right side.

May 31, 1942

OPINION: CAMPS ARE THE BEST SOLUTION FOR ALL INVOLVED

The attack on Pearl Harbor stunned all Americans, no doubt even those of Japanese descent. How could our government not have seen something like this coming? What else don't we know about this enemy?

Our Japanese American friends are certainly mostly good people. That is why it is even more important they accept relocation for the good of all of us. By complying, they can show their loyalty to the United States, and the US government can rest assured that any potential threats have been removed.

The process will be as quick and as safe as possible. Yes, many will be disturbed and inconvenienced. But this is a time of war. Aren't we all inconvenienced to some extent? With tensions high, the West Coast could become a place where Japanese Americans' lives are at risk. Anyone who could be seen as an enemy is in danger. Relocation is safest for the Japanese Americans.

May 31, 1942
Dear Diary,

Papa says that we must pack up and move to Poston without complaint. He thinks doing so will show that we are loyal American citizens, and hopes it means we will be released sooner. But I'm not sure I agree with him. By forcing us into a relocation center, they are taking away our basic rights, part of what American democracy was founded on. How can we be denied our rights as citizens simply because of our heritage?

Sumiko

"How can I pack our whole life into boxes in just a few days?" Sumiko's mama asked desperately, to no one in particular.

Sumiko didn't respond. She knew her mother wasn't looking for an answer, at least not really. This whole thing—

being forced into a prison camp simply because they were Japanese—didn't make any sense. *I was born here. My parents were too. Why are they treating us like we're the enemy?*

Sumiko opened the jewelry box and took out a gold-and-garnet ring that Obaasan had given her. Visiting her in Los Angeles seemed like such a long time ago.

"Keep this for good luck, Sumiko, dear," she'd told her. "I know you'll wear it well."

Sumiko sighed. She didn't want to take the ring into camp with her for fear she might lose it. Her mother had already sold most of their nice furniture to neighbors. Sumiko was helping her mama work through the rest of their belongings. They would put their sentimental items into a trunk and bring it to a storage facility.

Sumiko put her ring back in the small, brown box, and snapped it shut. She put it inside the trunk. She wiped a tear from her eye, thinking of her last day at Phoenix Elementary. Mrs. Fields had been sad to see her go—she even gave her books to take with her.

How is it that this war has divided my life so much in just a few short months?

The entire family was careful to obey all orders issued by the government. Her father even turned in his binoculars and camera over to the police station after Japanese Americans were told to turn in all "contraband."

Chapter Eleven

Dear Emi,

My family is all packed up and ready to go. I can't believe the day is already here. Everything has been so fast-paced preparing for our departure that I almost feel a sense of peace knowing we're leaving now. But I'm scared too. Will we ever see our home again?

Please write me often, will you? I promise I will write you.

Your friend,
Suzie

$\mathcal{I}$t was the Adachis' last supper at home. There was rice and chicken stew with everything in it: big chunks of potatoes and carrots, green bell peppers, celery, onions, and lots of thick pieces of meat. Sumiko's mama said the whole family needed to be well fed before the trip.

But they weren't going on vacation.

Papa reminded them that they couldn't worry about the rotting vegetable crops, the farm equipment, or the house, or how any of it would fair in their absence. For the moment, they had to concentrate on what was next. He said that he trusted George Findley, their neighbor, to harvest the crops and pay the rent with the money that he had given him.

Mama said that the Findleys and the Millers would eat what was left of the food in their pantry.

When the meal was over, Mama and Sumiko prepared food for the next day's journey. Mama wrapped peanut butter sandwiches in waxed paper and placed them in a box with some rice balls. Then she scrubbed and washed the rice pot and put it away in its place on the counter. She cleaned up the same as she did every night after dinner.

When the kitchen was spotless, Mama said, "Sumiko, go and get ready for bed now."

Sumiko was numb from the day's stresses and didn't want to take a bath, but she obeyed her mother.

She got a towel from the closet and her pajamas and went to their small bathroom. Then she soaked in peace, happy for the last moments of relaxation and rest.

"Oyasumi." *Good night*, Mama said.

Sumiko nodded and headed to her bedroom for her last night in her own bed.

What will happen to our house? Sumiko pulled the covers up tight around her chin. *Will our house look different when we return? What if we never come back?* Sumiko hoped that no one would look at the things they had packed away, their books and picture albums. All their clothes were also packed away in boxes. It didn't seem possible that they would live with only the few things that they could carry with them.

Sumiko thought about how much she'd miss Emi, and how unfair it was that Emi wasn't coming with her. Actually, there wasn't any part of this that was fair.

She lay in her bed staring at the ceiling, unable to sleep. She felt like a leaf blowing in the wind with no control over where she went.

PART II

Poston Relocation Center

Chapter Twelve

It was barely dawn, but the Adachi family car was packed and ready to go.

We are on our way to our prison home. Sumiko couldn't quite keep the irony out of her thoughts.

The family stopped at a gas station. Mr. Adachi had already made an arrangement with the young gasoline attendant, Willie, who they knew from years of frequenting the station, to buy their car. When Papa told Willie they needed to get to Poston first, Willie offered to drive them there.

After stretching her legs one last time, Sumiko climbed into the car. It was only a few hours until they reached their destination.

In the distance, in the middle of the vast, dry, flat land, hundreds of barracks enclosed by barbed wire came into view. Guard towers surrounded the compound. A huge black-and-white sign appeared, looking out of place in the expanse of desert: "Poston Indian Reservation."

They had arrived.

Willie stopped the car and helped the family unload their belongings. He pulled out his wallet and handed Mr. Adachi some cash—payment for the car.

Mr. Adachi quickly hid the cash in his shoes.

After giving Mr. Adachi a firm handshake, Willie got in the car and turned it back toward Phoenix.

Sumiko and her parents approached the gate, above which was the guard tower. The tower held two armed guards, who had their guns pointed at the incoming crowd. Sumiko couldn't feel her hands or feet; she walked in a daze. She'd never seen a gun before.

Sumiko snuck a side glance at the guards as she walked through the gate, hoping they wouldn't notice her. The white faces of the guards looked serious. The sign said to keep ten feet away from the fence in both English and

Japanese. Sumiko stood a little straighter, wanting to appear as if she were staying in line.

Sumiko gripped her father's hand a little tighter, and her mother walked a little behind them. Hundreds of weary people, arms loaded with bundles, coats, and babies, trudged through the open gates. It was getting dark already.

"Ganbare," she heard her mother say. *Persevere.*

It was a long, dusty walk to find a barrack that wasn't already filled. The dry dirt left by the bulldozers during construction was very deep in areas. Sumiko's feet sometimes sunk into the ground, making her feel like she was sinking into quicksand. There was not one blade of green grass, not one weed, and no trees. Everything was dirt and dust. After searching for a while, they found an unoccupied barrack.

Metal cots with thin gray-and-white mattresses were lined up on the black asphalt floor. A single light bulb hung from the rafters, casting long shadows around the room. Sumiko found a cot in the corner of the room and claimed it, setting her bag on top.

I guess I'm home, she thought grimly.

Chapter Thirteen

June 5, 1942
Dear Diary,

My name is Sumiko Adachi.

I live in Block 227, apartment 10-A in the Poston Relocation Center in Poston, Arizona.

My prisoner number is 22816-C.

Never mind that they call this place a relocation center. Make no mistake: I am in prison. The government says I am not a citizen anymore. I am a "non-alien."

Here's the truth: I am an American citizen, stripped of my constitutional rights. I am a prisoner in my own country. I sleep on a canvas cot under which is a suitcase with my life's belongings, a change of clothes, *a notebook, and a pencil. Why? I haven't done anything wrong. What will happen to me and my family?*

Sumiko

Clang! Clang! Clang! A sharp sound, like a rock hitting something metal, broke through the gray dullness of the room.

Sumiko ran to the door to see what all the commotion was about. People were hurrying back in the direction of the front gate.

"Time for chow! Mess hall," one of them said.

The last thing Sumiko wanted to do was eat. She hadn't had an appetite since she woke up this morning.

Her mama and papa were at her side now.

"We better go get some food. I don't know when they'll offer it next," her father said.

Sumiko thought back to their last dinner at home and choked back tears. She stepped outside in a half daze and followed her parents and the other prisoners down a long path, past five or six rows of barracks.

In the drab and dark interior of the mess hall, she saw silhouettes of a few helpers busily moving back and forth. The whole place had a strong smell of mutton stew. It made her nauseated.

At about five o'clock, the cook banged on the back of an aluminum pan with a smaller skillet; the first call for supper. Servers behind the counter dished out stew and rice. A few kids wrinkled their noses. Sumiko pushed her misery and homesickness away and joined her parents, who were helping to fill teapots and water pitchers.

When the work was done, her family got in line for their supper. They found a spot at a far table against the wall to eat. After a whole day of snacking on their prepared snacks, it felt good to Sumiko to sit down with her parents and eat together. She scooped the white rice untouched by the stew into her teacup. To her surprise, it tasted good. But it wasn't the same as her mother's cooking.

Sumiko looked around, surveying the room. *There are more people here than I thought.* The mess hall was like the other barracks except that it was not partitioned into separate rooms. It was hot and had an overwhelming and unappetizing smell that was almost suffocating.

Mama tried to joke with Sumiko about some sashimi for the rice, but Sumiko couldn't make herself crack a smile. The leftover bread with milk and raisins wasn't bad, but she couldn't tolerate the mutton. Mama must have thought the same thing. She hated to waste food, but she hardly touched it.

When dinner was over, everyone headed back to the barracks. Sumiko was full but in a daze. *This still doesn't feel real.*

When they got back to their barrack, Papa checked on the money he had smuggled in with his bedroll. Mama brought in a wet towel from the shower barrack so they could all wipe their faces.

Sumiko's mattress was dusty but she was too tired to carry it outside to shake out the dust. They spread out their bedrolls, glad for the opportunity to rest. Papa made a quick trip to the men's shower, and Mama organized the family clothes for tomorrow. Curfew was ten o'clock and they made it under their covers just in time.

Sumiko thought of Emi at home in her own bed. *I have to write her soon,* she thought. *Does she miss me?*

The night was warm and still, and the camp was silent. Sumiko couldn't hear any sounds from insects, birds, dogs barking, or cars driving by. *It's so different from the farm.*

Every so often, huge searchlights shone through the small windows, throwing unfamiliar shadows against the unfinished walls.

Sumiko couldn't shake the feeling that she was being watched.

Clang! Clang! Clang!

Sumiko jolted awake at the sound of the mess hall bell. Outside the barrack door, hundreds of people hurried toward the sound. Sumiko and her parents dressed and hurried out the door to follow.

At the mess hall, Sumiko went through the line for pancakes, Spam, and stewed prunes.

After breakfast, the shower, laundry, and latrine bustled with activity. Mothers lined up with clothes to wash. Mama, too, had a bundle of laundry wrapped up in a sheet.

Sumiko dragged her straw mattress out into the open desert to shake out the straw. When she returned to the barrack, the heat was unbearable. At about 120 degrees, the black tar-paper walls caused the air inside the barracks to be so insufferable that it seemed like it could have boiled a pot of water. Papa finally relented.

"Tonight, we will sleep outside," he told them.

Sumiko could hardly wait until nighttime.

When the sky darkened, Sumiko carried her cot and sheet outside wearing her loose cotton nightdress. Prisoners, young and old, lined up at the outside faucet carrying their cots. Sumiko placed her cot under the faucet and sloshed the running water back and forth over the canvas surface.

They decided to sleep along the west side of their barrack. Sumiko's whole body relaxed as it hit the cooled cot.

A falling star steaked across the sky, and the prisoners *ooh*ed and *aah*ed with delight.

One by one, quiet fell upon their tired bodies and the children drifted off to sleep. Eerie howls of a coyote floated into camp. Even in the night outside, the oppressive heat was unrelenting.

Sumiko slept, waking several hours later bone dry and hot. The coyote howls sounded closer. Just before dawn, she heard the coyotes as they rushed through her block. Sumiko lay frozen in terror. But no one else moved, either, and the animals moved on to the next block.

Chapter Fourteen

May 26, 1942

RELOCATION OF JAPANESE THREATENS THOUSANDS OF ACRES OF CROPS

With thousands of Japanese American farmers locked away in camps, who is left to tend their crops? That's the question the US government is asking as more than 225,000 acres stand to go to waste if no action is taken soon.

Six thousand farms were left abandoned in the wake of the relocation of Japanese Americans that began in February. Thus far, only 1,000 farmers have offered to take over the land. The farms alone, without the crops included, are worth upwards of $70 million.

Whoever takes over the farms must keep up the crops, as these resources are too valuable to waste. Reports have been received that new owners have turned over the fields and destroyed the crops, which is an act of sabotage.

June 15, 1942
Dear Diary,

Papa has become friendly with one of the camp directors, Mr. Rockland. Mr. Rockland says that a manager has to be appointed for our block, and it could be Papa!

According to administration rules, a block manager has to be a citizen. Since Papa is a Nisei he qualifies. But he does not speak Japanese, which Mr. Rockland says is helpful with Issei prisoners.

Doesn't it seem a little odd that they say we are non-aliens, but that one has to be a citizen to be a block manager?

Sumiko

June 21, 1942
Dear Diary,

I am eleven now; my birthday was yesterday. Only Mama remembered my birthday. But it wasn't until suppertime. She said suddenly, "Today is your birthday, isn't it?"

There were no cake or presents, but I didn't expect those things anyway. Maybe next year. I hope we'll be home by then.

Sumiko

July 2, 1942
Dear Diary,

Mama keeps telling me to drink more water. She's worried about the heat getting to me. But the water has a strong metallic taste, so I drink tea instead.

Sumiko

Dear Emi,

I finally can write to you with some good news!
Mama told me that she is going to have a baby.
I'm so excited to have a little baby brother or
sister. You know that I've always wanted to be a
big sister. But I'm nervous about a baby living here
with us. The baby will be born a prisoner. What
kind of life will it have?

I hope I will see you soon.

Suzie

Dear Suzie,

I miss you so much! I made my dad drive past your farm the other day. It looked so empty, and I started to cry. I hope you are doing okay.

I've been learning new dance moves, and I wish you were here to play the piano for me. I'm not very good yet, but I'm working hard. When you get back, we can start our Hollywood-bound act!

Miss you!
Emi

August 6, 1942
Dear Diary,

There is a little boy in camp who follows me around. His name is Masahiro. He asks me questions like, "Why can't we go home?" Or, "How come he has a gun?" How do I explain to him that we are imprisoned? He'll only ask more questions: Are we bad people? What did we do to deserve this?

    Whenever he asks me questions, I try to change the subject. Sometimes I suggest we go exploring instead. I always make sure to keep a respectful distance from the guards when we go exploring, though. Usually, as we go, other children join us along the way. I feel like the Pied Piper of Hamlin since I'm the oldest girl in the group of children.

Sumiko

Dear Emi,

School started a couple days ago. When I left Phoenix I wasn't sure if I would ever go to school again, but I am glad to have something to keep my mind on. I am so happy to be learning again that school here almost seems normal.

It's held in an empty barrack space. Miss Tanaka is great; she's smart and the other students seem to love her too.

Yesterday I went to the gravel pit and got some rocks. Miss Tanaka warned us to be careful about touching any animals around here because of diseases. She told us about a tarantula in one of the barracks. We are going to see it tomorrow and I'm very excited.

It's sad that I'm getting used to living here, but what choice do I have? At the very least, I have settled into a routine.

Suzie

September 21, 1942
Dear Diary,

Blocks 3, 6, 12, 23 had no running water this morning because the water pipe broke. The people in these blocks had to go to other places to wash their faces and brush their teeth. It took twice as long because of the crowds!

Sumiko

October 18, 1942
Dear Diary,

There are a lot of birthdays around here lately.

It was Bobby's birthday yesterday. He lives in the barrack next to ours. Bobby turned nine years old. To celebrate, he made a kite that flew very high. But his brother, Johnny, cried when he didn't have a kite. So Bobby made one for him too.

We all wrote letters to Miss Tanaka because today was her birthday. My classmate Tomomi played a joke on her this afternoon. He put a bug on her chair after she got up. When she saw it she screamed and jumped really high.

I've made a few friends, but I still miss Emi. I miss her loud laugh. I wish I was still sitting outside her family's store with her, dreaming of our futures.

Sumiko

October 24, 1942
Dear Diary,

Sickness is really becoming a problem around here. Miki's little brother had pneumonia. I notice Papa is not so well either. All of us are cold at night because there is no insulation from the cold or heat. I am getting sick of the food. We don't have any fresh vegetables; they're all canned.

I hope Mama and her baby stay healthy. Only a few more months until I get to meet my new brother or sister.

Sumiko

November 9, 1942
Dear Diary,

Everybody knows everything about everybody—when you go to the shower room, when you go to the latrine, how long you are in the latrine, and on and on. You can't keep anything private in a place like this. But hardly anyone pays attention to what anyone wears. There's no point. None of us have many clothes. We all came with what we could carry. Our bodies are covered by desert dirt every day by mid-afternoon. Everyone just keeps washing and mending the same clothes. The laundry room is never empty.

Mama is constantly mending clothes. No matter when I come in, she is sitting on her cot with a needle and thread, sometimes resting her hand on her growing belly. If only she had her sewing machine . . .

Sumiko

Chapter Fifteen

It wasn't long before the camp administration set aside a plot of land at the edge of camp for farming. It was decided that prisoners would do the manual labor of tending to the crops. Laborers were paid wages of twelve dollars per month for eight hours of work daily. At first, the administration said machinery could only be operated by white personnel. But eventually they allowed the prisoners to take over all the farming. The prisoners proved to be better at using the machinery than the white personnel, anyway. After all, many of them, including Sumiko's father, had their own farms back home.

Sumiko's father and others worked to prepare the land for farming. But they faced many challenges along the way, the first being farming in an unfamiliar territory.

Initially, the dry land and lack of water posed problems for cultivation. But eventually a large-scale irrigation system

was installed. It brought water directly from the Colorado River, only two and a half miles away, to the crops.

The farmers also battled dust storms. It seemed to Sumiko that her father and the others were constantly plowing the land in an attempt to reshape the landscape and bring fresh, fertile soil to the top.

The camp farm cultivated a variety of fresh vegetables, including some traditional Japanese vegetables such as daikon and gobo from seeds the prisoners had brought with them.

Sumiko was overjoyed that they would have fresh vegetables to eat, and even more grateful because she knew how much work her father and the other farmers had done to make that food possible. But her father told her that much of the crop would be sold for commercial use or distributed to American troops.

INMATE STRIKE ENDS AT ARIZONA RELOCATION CENTER

The inmate strike at the Poston Relocation Center is over, ten days after the beating of an alleged informant at Camp I.

The November 14 incident resulted in two prisoners being held by the camp administration without a trial. Camp I inmates held protests and tried to negotiate a peaceful settlement, but talks with the camp administrators stalled and workers went on strike on November 19.

Inmates demanded that they be given more of a role in communicating with the administration. Poston has been the site of previous strife, with inmates fighting for better wages and conditions. When the camp administration announced that only Nisei could serve on an inmate advisory board, the inmates formed their own board on which Issei could also serve.

A compromise was reached on November 24 that brought the strike to an end. It was based on cooperation between inmates and leaders, and the prisoners are expected to have more of a say in their conditions going forward.

Chapter Sixteen

December 7, 1942
Dear Diary,

I miss my room where I could read and write and watch the moonlight through my window and just be by myself. I miss the sound of cicadas buzzing at night on our farm. Right now, I can hear people talking through our thin wall and other sounds a few more walls down. I wish I could have some space to myself.

And I can't believe I'm saying this, but I miss the warmth. It gets very cold here at night. Sometimes it doesn't warm up until noon! I miss Emi too.

Sumiko

Dear Emi,

My baby brother is dead. I know you didn't even
know that Mama had her baby, or that it was a
boy, or that his name was Keiji. But none of that
matters now because he's gone.

He came one month earlier than he was
supposed to. When Mama got to the hospital,
the nurse said the doctor was not there. He had
collapsed during the night from exhaustion. He had
delivered two babies and had been on his feet all
that time without help. So he had gone back to the
barracks to sleep.

Mama was in a room by herself most of the
time, and was in labor for almost twenty-eight
hours. A nurse would come in every once in a while
to check on her and the baby. At one point, the
nurse said that the baby's heartbeat was very
faint and that she was going to have to call the
doctor. But Mama waited for a long time for the

doctor to come check on her. When he finally did, he told her that they would have to pull the baby out of her using a pincer-type instrument called forceps.

Mama says she remembers looking at Keiji after he was born and thinking something didn't look right. He was very pale and his cries were very faint. When I finally got to see him, a few hours after he was born, I noticed that he had scabs on his head where the forceps had been used.

Later that evening he was taken to the nursery to sleep. In the morning, a nurse informed us that he had died overnight. I had never seen Mama cry like she did at that moment. She screamed and fell to the floor.

I know I said that this place is no place for a baby, but that didn't mean I didn't want my baby brother.

Suzie

Chapter Seventeen

Dear Suzie,

I'm so sorry to hear about your baby brother. I hope your mama is okay. I miss you so much.

I am still dancing even though I'm not on the dance team this year. I didn't make the team. I'm really disappointed. I practiced so hard. Mama thinks it's because I'm Japanese. I think she's right. But, I'm trying not to let this setback stop me. I got some books to use at home. I'm using them to learn the ballet steps as best I can, but it's hard without someone to guide you.

I hope you'll continue writing to me. I wonder when you'll be able to come home. I hope it's soon.

Love,
Emi

US ARMY ORGANIZES ALL-JAPANESE 442ND REGIMENTAL COMBAT TEAM

Thousands of Japanese American volunteers, some of them coming from behind the walls of confinement camps, will soon be on their way to Mississippi for US Army basic training. The mostly-Hawaiian crew will form the 442nd Regimental Combat Team, composed entirely of Japanese Americans with some white officers.

The regiment has been in the works for several months as the United States is in need of soldiers to support the war in the Atlantic. But the notion of bringing Japanese American soldiers into the military was controversial. It required a reversal of the Army's position that Japanese American men were not to be drafted.

One safeguard the Army has implemented is a loyalty questionnaire. All internees must answer the questionnaire, including the military volunteers. It is designed to test the loyalty of the respondent. Sample questions include whether one wished to serve in combat and if he or she renounced the Emperor of Japan.

"*O*hayo gozaimasu." *Good morning.*

After having been in camp for over a year, the prisoners at Poston fell into a rhythm.

The Issei greeted one other with a nod. Strangers were no longer strangers.

"Atsui desu ne?" *It is hot, isn't it?*

The prisoners empathized with one another. Everyone was equal, whether they were lawyers or engineers or farmworkers or mothers. Mutual imprisonment had leveled the social classes that stood out in American society.

Chapter Eighteen

December 23, 1943

JAPANESE AMERICAN
CITIZENS LEAGUE PROVIDES
TOYS FOR CAMP CHILDREN

The National Japanese American Citizens League is doing whatever it can to make sure children in relocation centers have a merry Christmas this season. The organization has worked with several churches and other organizations to provide toys and gifts to more than 40,000 children.

The Citizens League dates back to the early 1930s, and has been especially active during wartime to help displaced Japanese American families. Planning for this Christmas season started three months ago, and more and more gifts are arriving every day from as far away as Canada.

Gifts will be distributed to each camp and then passed out by community organizers there.

Dear Emi,

Well, it looks like I'm spending another Christmas in this camp. Even though it's not like Christmas on our farm in Phoenix, everyone does their best to make the season as enjoyable and memorable as possible. I even helped decorate the mess hall last week!

School is coming along, but I miss our teacher Miss Tanaka. Mr. Fukuoka is so strict. Our final tests will be in May but that seems a long way off.

Keep practicing your dancing!

Suzie

"Sumiko, what do you want for Christmas this year?" Mama asked. Sumiko knew her parents had little to give her, but her mama had always managed to get her something special in years past.

"I'd like something to write and draw in," Sumiko said after a few moments. Her old notebook was almost completely full.

It was Christmas Eve, and the camp staff was sponsoring a pageant called *There Came Three Wise Men*. Sumiko had been anticipating the performance for weeks.

It did not disappoint. There was dancing and singing that floated into the night air. And after the performance, there was a party. It was one of the best days that Sumiko had had since she first came to the camp.

The next morning, Sumiko woke to find a notebook had been slipped under her pillow.

Dear Suzie,

Christmas was empty and sad this year because I don't have any close friends to share it with. People at school are still mean to me. Mama did her best to bring the Christmas spirit into our house. She bought a small nativity to place in the middle of our living room table. Tiny statues of Mary, Joseph, and baby Jesus were surrounded by animals and the three wise men. It was beautiful and peaceful.

Mama says that although the world has gone crazy, the Christmas story is always the same, and I know she's right in a way. I also think about how everything just starts again after Christmas.

I guess it's important to remember that, although that's easy for me to say as I sit in my house and you sit in a prison camp.

I wish things were different. I miss you.

Love,
Emi

Chapter Nineteen

Dear Suzie,

Something terrible has happened. Someone set fire to our store last night. Mama's urgent shouting woke me and Papa up early.

"Fire! Help! Fire!" she shouted.

I tried to shake off sleep from my eyes as Mama told me we had to get out of the house quickly. The air was thick with smoke and I tried to cover my face as I rushed upstairs and out the door. I was still in my bedclothes and had bare feet.

We raced across the street to the drugstore to call the fire department. Papa banged his palm on the glass until Mr. Johnson, the owner, appeared.

"Help!" "Fire!" "Hurry!" we all shouted together.

Mr. Johnson made the call while Mama, Papa, and I all huddled together away from the flames.

It was then that I saw it. Written across the front of our store in spray paint was: JAPS NOT WANTED.

The firefighters put out the blaze quickly, pouring great streams of water on the shooting flames. Then they checked carefully to make sure that the last spark was out.

There was broken glass everywhere and the whole store was flooded with water. Smoke had blackened the walls, most of the shelves were charred, and the counter was a black island of burned wood. Food in bags had been burned, the labels crinkled and peeling. Everything that wasn't in tins or cans was useless.

Papa isn't sure if we will close for good or not. Mama says "ganbare," and that we won't let anyone force us out.

We're moving a few blocks over to live with my aunt for now. I can't believe our home and business is ruined. Why would someone do this to us?

Mournfully,
Emi

Chapter Twenty

January 23, 1944

MEDICAL CARE IN RELOCATION CENTERS REMAINS A CHALLENGE, WITH SOME SUCCESSES

Shortages of medical supplies and staff have plagued Japanese American relocation centers, and those issues continue now nearly two years on. With more than 120,000 people to care for, resources are stretched more than ever. But staff soldier on despite the logistical challenges.

Quality of care is also a concern. Rather than a well-stocked hospital, care centers in camps are more like military first-aid tents where cleanliness is secondary. Camps have experienced outbreaks of disease and infection. Overcrowding just multiplies the problems.

While emergency treatment is suspect, those with ongoing medical conditions are at risk of not receiving proper care. Specialists can be hard to find. And as the War Relocation Authority has begun to allow some physicians to return to their practices outside the camps, staffing levels can be inconsistent.

One area of success has been dental care. Dental patients have relatively short wait times and there are plenty of dentists for the number of patients.

Dear Emi,

I'm so sorry to hear about your family's store. I hope that you can rebuild quickly. Please be careful. I worry about your family all the time.

I don't have anything but bad news to share. Papa hasn't been well so we took him to the doctor today. They said he's suffering from melancholia. They have no way of treating him here at camp, but we could arrange for him to go to the Phoenix Sanitarium where he can get shock treatments and maybe he'll come out of it. But we have to pay for it.

We had some money from the sale of the car so Mama said okay. I hope he comes home soon.

Suzie

Dear Emi,

I go to the sanitarium as often as I can to see Papa. But his body is deteriorating and it is painful to see. He looks swollen and has uncontrollable bouts of coughing.

Waiting patients look at us with pity, and the staff seem uncaring. Papa never criticizes, but we complain that he cannot tolerate sitting upright in a wheelchair for long periods of time. I can tell he is exhausted after each visit with us.

Suzie

May 5, 1944
Dear Diary,

Papa has been in the hospital for going on two months now. Yesterday he said to me, "I want you to go on and be the wonderful daughter to your mother that you've been to me."

This really scared me. He made it sound like he was dying.

He hardly looks like the man I used to know—the one who cultivated a farm from nothing. Most days he stays in bed, a pillow propped behind his back. His has become weak and is always tired.

I read to him every time we visit, and Mama holds his hand. The doctors aren't talking much to us. He can no longer use the chopsticks we bring him.

Sumiko

Dear Emi,

I feel like I'm living in a nightmare. First we lost Keiji, and now Papa.

Two days ago, we got word that we needed to go see Papa right away. We went to be with him and he passed away a short time after we arrived.

We talked to the doctor yesterday who told us, "He didn't really have melancholia. It was brought on by his heart." Papa had never had trouble with his heart before. He was only thirty-three years old.

His death certificate says he died from heart disease.

I can't help but wonder if we were never in camp, if Papa would still be with me today.

Suzie

Sumiko and her mother arranged for clearance to have a small funeral for Papa at the nearby Glendale cemetery.

"Don't cry, Sumiko. Your papa was grateful for the time he had in this world," Mama said. "We will be okay."

But Mama's words were little comfort to Sumiko. Sumiko felt so empty. Only the quiet was peaceful.

"Do not worry," Mama continued. "We need to remember your papa's memory."

Sumiko knew her mother was trying to be brave for her sake. But she was too devastated to even pretend it was working. Her father was gone.

He taught me to love all of life. And now he has no more life left to live.

July 27, 1944
Dear Diary,

I know I am an American. Even though I've been in this camp for two years, the shock of it all never goes away. I am a loyal American citizen who is incarcerated and treated like a criminal.

    I am angry that my government would do this to me. If I wasn't sent here, we never would have lost my baby brother and my father. My family can never recover from those losses.

                               Sumiko

Chapter Twenty-One

Dear Suzie,

I could not believe your last letter. I'm so sad for you and your mother. Your father was a great man.

Things are changing in my life. I'm on a train on my way to New York. We are moving there. Papa got offered a job in a big supermarket. I hope it will be better than Arizona.

I've seen so many places I never thought I'd see on this train, and I wish you could see them too. Texas was really big, but also desolate and dry. Every morning when I wake up, the terrain has changed. The fields in Indiana were so much different than Arizona. But we're getting closer to New York City now. There are so many houses here. Soon we'll change trains for somewhere called Barrytown where we're going to live.

I hope it will be a fresh start, but I'm sad to be farther away from you.

Emi

Chapter Twenty-Two

December 18, 1944

PRESIDENT ROOSEVELT LIFTS IMPRISONMENT OF JAPANESE AMERICANS

Though maintaining that the evacuation was "warranted," Major General Henry C. Pratt announced the end of the US military policy of Japanese American confinement. Public Proclamation No. 21 states that effective January 2, 1945, Japanese American prisoners from the West Coast may return to their homes. Pratt is commanding general of the Western Defense Command, based at the Presidio in San Francisco.

Pratt's order means that for more than 110,000 persons of Japanese ancestry, two-thirds of whom are American citizens, their wartime imprisonment will soon be over. Some restrictions will still be in place once they return, such as curfew times in certain areas. The proclamation cited "substantial improvement" in the war effort as a reason to end the imprisonment now.

And today in Washington, the US Supreme Court is expected to rule in Korematsu v. United States. Fred Korematsu, of Oakland, California, has challenged the legality of Executive Order 9066, which began the process of Japanese American relocation.

PART III

Home Again

Chapter Twenty-Three

Sumiko wasn't sure why she was feeling a twinge of sadness. It was January of 1945, and she and her mother were free to leave Poston Relocation Center.

While she packed up her belongings, she felt a mix of emotions: happy and excited to see her family's farm again but also anxious and sorrowful. Her father was not coming with them.

It had been almost three years since they arrived at the barren, desolate camp. *Had it really been that long?* Sumiko thought. It seemed like so much had changed during that time.

"What do you think home will look like now?" Sumiko asked Mama.

A thoughtful look came over Mama's face. "I'm not sure. But we must put the past behind us and try to pick up where we left off."

Sumiko knew that would be hard to do. Her father wouldn't be with them, for starters. The farm had been in Mr. Findley's hands since they left, and there was no telling the state that it would be in now. And Emi had moved away.

The two made their way to the departure station. Mama smiled and squeezed Sumiko's hand. After a while, the two bounced along in the back seat of a bus as it headed down the long, dusty road.

This was the day Sumiko had been waiting for, here at last.

Sumiko's heart skipped a beat and she pinched her leg to see if she was dreaming. *Is it true? Am I home?*

Sumiko found she was actually a little self-conscious standing in front of her family's farmhouse. *It's like we're strangers to this place.* It had been almost three years since she last stood here. Still, there was something warm and comforting about the familiar, brown dirt and the worn, gray shutters that put her at ease.

An older, grayer Mr. Miller greeted Sumiko and her mother at the door.

"Welcome home," he said, smiling.

Mr. Miller let them inside. Mr. Findley was there, too, and dinner was waiting for them.

The group talked over a late-night dinner. The farm was doing well. Mr. Findley's son had helped labor in the fields while they were away, and it was decided that he would continue to do so for the time being, as would Mr. Sanchez, another man who was brought on to help in the fields. Sumiko and Mama would help as much as they could too.

The reunited neighbors didn't talk about Papa's death. Sumiko appreciated that.

February 8, 1945
Dear Diary,

These past few days it's been very quiet around here.

I asked Mama if we could go to Emi's store because I wanted to see it. I sort of wish I hadn't. I know her family was so proud of that store, and seeing it still in ruins made me cry. Mama said, "After the rain falls, the ground hardens." I think she was trying to tell me that the Kunos will come out of this ordeal stronger than they were before. I hope that's true. But I still wish Emi were here.

While we were in town I mailed the birthday present I made Emi. I miss her so much. I don't have any friends since returning home. Her family is coming to visit for Thanksgiving, and I wish I didn't have to wait so long.

Speaking of New York, Mama is talking about moving there in a few years. It'll be tough to keep up with farmwork with Papa gone. I'm not sure if I want to move or not. Part of me thinks that if we do, I'll lose all memory of Papa. But I also want to be in a better place, and hopefully we'd move close to Emi's family.

More than anything, I want to feel like I belong. I don't feel like I belong anywhere right now.

Sumiko

Dear Suzie,

I am so happy to hear that you are free of that horrible place! I wish I was still in Phoenix to welcome you home!

My new middle school offers some courses for learning to speak Japanese. I'm thinking of signing up, but I want to dance too.

Overall I think I like it here, but it's so different than Phoenix! And I am still getting used to the weather. It snows! Papa works at a large supermarket and Mama has been busy setting up our new house and helping me organize my school schedule. The newness of everything can get me down sometimes. I think about Kuno's Market often, and that makes me sad.

I've been able to see a few movies on breaks from my studies. Doesn't it sound like I'm living a wild life? Can't wait to see you for Thanksgiving!

Love,
Emi

Chapter Twenty-Four

$\mathcal{N}$ot long after returning to Phoenix, Sumiko bought a large, white drawing tablet on a shopping trip. She also picked up some charcoal pencils. The world looked different to her now, after the long years of confinement. She wanted—no, she *needed*—to record what she saw.

When she got home she sat at her kitchen table, unsure of where to start. She looked up at her mother as she worked to prepare dinner. Sumiko saw the determined line of her eyebrow, the graying of her hair around her temples, and her weathered hands.

Before she knew what she was doing, Sumiko opened to a fresh page in her notebook and started sketching. First it was her mother's hands; they told a story. In them, Sumiko could see the hours she had toiled on the farm, turning the barren land into rich soil. She saw the thin, weathered wedding band that her father had given Mama.

She flipped the page. Next was her mother's face. As she drew, Sumiko saw a bit of herself in her mother that she hadn't noticed before. The shape of her eyes, the curve of her nose, the set of her jaw.

Sumiko focused on her drawings for weeks. She was inspired by everything around her. She saw the old piano in the living room with new eyes. The fence outside their house was no longer just weathered; its texture suggested years of endurance and fortitude.

One afternoon, Mama walked by Sumiko, who was deep into another drawing. A smile flickered across Mama's face. "Maybe you'll go east to art college, Sumiko," she said.

"You mean, you want to leave?" Sumiko asked. "But we just got here."

"It is in your blood, you know," her mother said.

"What is?"

"Your great-great grandfather was a well-known woodblock painter from Kyoto. His name was Ichiro Hiromi," Mama said, as she began to put pieces of wood into the fireplace.

Sumiko was speechless. *Why have I never heard of him before?*

"You could draw what it means to be a survivor. Paint your experiences for future generations to see," Mama said.

Sumiko saw the strength in her mother's eyes. *We are both survivors.* Sumiko knew she needed to live her life as best she could. She couldn't get back the years that she'd lost, but she could move forward.

Later that evening, Sumiko said good night to Mama and went to her room.

She sat down at the edge of her bed with her notepad on her lap. She drew until her eyes were weary. She felt a special connection to the artist relative she had never met, knowing there was a love of beauty running through the family.

When she finally crept into bed, she noticed how the shapes and shadows in the room were now familiar and comforting to her. She said a prayer, hoping that she had gotten through the worst, and that the best was ahead.

One gray Arizona summer day, Sumiko was outside with her drawing pad. Suddenly, she heard the kitchen door slam, and her mama came running out.

"It's over!" she yelled, running toward her daughter and waving a kitchen towel frantically. "It's really over. Japan's surrendered. The war is over!"

Sumiko threw her notepad off her lap. "It is?" Sumiko cheered and hugged her mother.

Her mother wasn't done yet. She ran down their dirt driveway shouting to anybody who would listen.

"Have you heard? The war is over!"

August 16, 1945

JAPAN TO SURRENDER ENDING WAR IN PACIFIC

In a radio broadcast to the nation, Japanese Emperor Hirohito announced to his people that Japan will accept the Potsdam Declaration and formally surrender to the Allies, bringing to an end a long and painful conflict in the Pacific.

After Germany's surrender in May, all attention had turned to the Pacific theater, where Japan originally showed no sign of surrender. But Japanese resistance crumbled with stunning speed after the first atomic bombs mushroomed over Hiroshima on August 6 and Nagasaki on August 9. The reeling Japanese government survived a brief coup attempt, with Hirohito ultimately deciding to surrender.

While the emperor has agreed in principle, the formal surrender will occur at a later date. This effectively brings to a close a conflict that has enveloped the globe for six-and-a-half years and the United States since the attack on Pearl Harbor on December 7, 1941.

EPILOGUE

Chapter Twenty-Five

The short days slipped quickly now into long, cool nights. The leaves turned brown and fluttered to the ground with the chilly winds that blew in from the desert.

Sumiko's life had started to settle into a routine. With Thanksgiving came a feeling of anticipation in the air. This was Sumiko's first Thanksgiving since they had been released from prison.

They had many friends coming to celebrate with them. Emi and her parents were coming to visit. And Sumiko had good news to share: she and her mother would be moving to New York City that spring. Mama had also invited Mr. Miller and his family to Thanksgiving dinner since she was so grateful for his help and support. Mama said there is no doubt that they would have lost their farm if it weren't for Mr. Miller.

Finally, the day was here. Sumiko's face was glued to the front window when Emi and her parents' car pulled up the driveway. Sumiko raced out of the house, leapt over the porch steps, and clobbered Emi in a giant hug just as her friend emerged from the car.

"Emi!" she screamed. "It's really you!"

"I missed you so much, Suzie!" Emi said with tears running down her face. She looked different to Sumiko, more grown up.

"I missed you too! And we're moving to New York City!" Sumiko blurted out in her excitement.

Emi's face went from happy to completely giddy. "Really? That's great!"

Sumiko hugged Emi again. She'd waited so long, but she finally had her best friend back.

Inside, there were flowers on the table, and Mama had baked a pumpkin pie. Sumiko had decorated the table with special plates from their trunk of treasures.

Sumiko couldn't remember the last time she had seen such a wonderful dinner. The roast turkey their neighbor Helen White carried in from the kitchen was plump, brown, and glistening on its bed of parsley. It was the biggest turkey Sumiko had ever seen. And with it came candied sweet potatoes, string beans, carrots, and a beautiful cranberry salad.

As the group sat together around the big table, there was such a good feeling of closeness, common culture, and sharing that Sumiko already knew that she didn't ever want the day to end.

Sumiko's mother sat at the head of the table, her face calm and full of peace and gratitude. She began to speak, thanking their guests for coming and for their support over the last several years. She talked about how difficult things had been in the prison camp.

Mama never talks this much, thought Sumiko.

"But I will forgive them for what they did to all of us," Mama said, looking at Sumiko.

Sumiko looked down, wondering if she really could forgive those who had hurt her.

"I know we've had reasons for much anger," Mama continued, "but we won't destroy ourselves with any more bitterness."

Sumiko nodded slowly. She didn't feel ready to forgive, maybe she never would, but she was glad her mother had found some peace after everything that had happened to them.

"Forgiveness takes a bundle of hate off your back," Mama continued. "There are ways to fight back without destroying yourself or others."

The table was silent as they listened to every word that left Mama's mouth. Emi looked at Suzie and smiled. She understood.

"We're survivors, and we'll struggle to rebuild our lives. But we also cherish this life that we have. With so much tragedy around us, we will move forward to pursue our dreams and remain strong."

Mama raised her glass. "Kanpai."

"Kanpai," the group said in unison. *Cheers.*

Author's Note

The preceding is a work of fiction. However, the experiences of Sumiko Adachi were very real for thousands of Americans during World War II.

What the US government called Military Area No. 1 was simply "home" for the 120,000 Japanese Americans who had lived in a huge swath of the United States from Washington to Arizona. Any person of Japanese descent could be forced to leave everything behind and move to a prison camp. This all happened in just a few months following the Japanese attack on Pearl Harbor in December 1941. But while that may have been the direct cause, there were in reality many contributing factors that began decades earlier.

Anti-Asian sentiment had been present in America since the 1800s. The influx of Chinese laborers in the California Gold Rush established their population in the West, which was met with hatred and distrust from white settlers. This hatred was later made official with laws that barred Asian immigrants from holding certain jobs or owning land in certain states. This eventually resulted in the ending of immigration from Asia. By the 1900s, this anti-Asian sentiment was turned toward Japanese Americans.

In Sumiko's Arizona, anti-Japanese sentiment was as rampant as it was on the West Coast. In 1913, Arizona became one of the first states to pass alien land laws, which prevented certain people who were ineligible for citizenship from buying farmland, and specifically targeted the Japanese. Arizona put further restrictions on Japanese farmers in 1921, passing a law that prevented them from renting land. But Japanese farm families found ways around the laws and thrived despite the restrictions. Agriculture was one of the main ways that Japanese Americans made a living. This upset many white farmers in the area, who worked throughout the 1930s to harass and intimidate Japanese farmers and their families.

Another factor in the increasing hatred of Japanese Americans was the Empire of Japan's growing military power and influence. As Japan grew to be more of a threat, some saw these "foreigners" in a new way: as the enemy. After Pearl Harbor, a string of surprise Japanese victories in the Pacific fueled those irrational fears. Famously, in the aftermath of Pearl Harbor, US Secretary of the Navy Frank Knox warned of a "fifth column" of Japanese conspirators waiting to destroy the United States from within.

Simmering historical hatred of the Japanese boiled over into extraordinary fear and distrust following Pearl Harbor. Japanese Americans were accused of spying against and sabotaging the United States. Arrests were made mere hours after the attack took place and continued into 1942. The notion of exiling Japanese Americans, promoted by Knox and others, became a very real possibility. On February 19, 1942, President Franklin D. Roosevelt signed Executive Order 9066, giving the military the authority to expel and imprison any person that it deemed the enemy.

In Arizona, that included approximately 650 Japanese Americans in the Phoenix area. Most of these people were American-born, which by law would make them US citizens. Arizona was included in Military Area No. 1 when it was created in March of 1942. Many Japanese Americans living in Arizona reported directly to a prison camp (known by the government as a "relocation center") in the Arizona desert, oftentimes driving themselves, like

Sumiko and her family did. However, in other states, most Japanese Americans were forced to report to temporary prison camps before being sent on to more permanent ones. The army thought that immediate imprisonment of Japanese Americans was necessary, thus prisoners stayed in these temporary prison camps (called "assembly centers") an average of three months while permanent prison camps were constructed.

The dividing line of Military Area No. 1 cut entire communities in two. In Phoenix, families who happened to live on opposite sides of the street were separated. The ones who got to stay had the relief of not being forced into a confinement camp. But they lived with the fear of not knowing if they would be next. They also drew the anger and suspicion of the non-Japanese population. In a way, they were prisoners in their own homes.

During World War II, the constitutionality of confinement was tested in a few cases. *Ex parte Endo* was ruled on in December 1944. While the court did not rule on whether confinement was constitutional, it ruled that the government lacked the authority to imprison citizens that it could not prove were disloyal. This ended confinement, though Executive Order 9066 wasn't formally rescinded until 1976.

A separate case, *Korematsu v. United States*, judged the same day as *Endo*, ruled that the order was constitutional. But this case has since been subject to scrutiny despite remaining a legal precedent. In 1980, The Commission on Wartime Relocation and Internment of Civilians was convened by Congress to investigate the events that led to Executive Order 9066. It concluded that there was no legal or moral basis for Japanese confinement, and that the evacuation had been caused by "race prejudice, war hysteria, and a failure of political leadership."

The report made recommendations of reparations. These included a payment of $20,000 to each person imprisoned and a formal apology from the United States government. The apology was signed into law by President Ronald Reagan in 1988.

The *Korematsu* ruling received a measure of retraction in 2018. In a review of a related case, Chief Justice John Roberts cited *Korematsu* as "gravely wrong" and having "no place in law under the Constitution." While Korematsu's case is still legally on the books, Roberts' retraction makes it clear that this period in American history was illegal and shameful.

Japanese Americans had to leave their homes, businesses, farms, and fishing boats behind when the War Relocation Authority forced them into confinement camps.

The Mochida family awaits evacuation in California. Each person was given an identification tag in an attempt to keep the family together.

Poston, Arizona

Christmas at the Granada Relocation Center in Amache, Colorado

Timeline

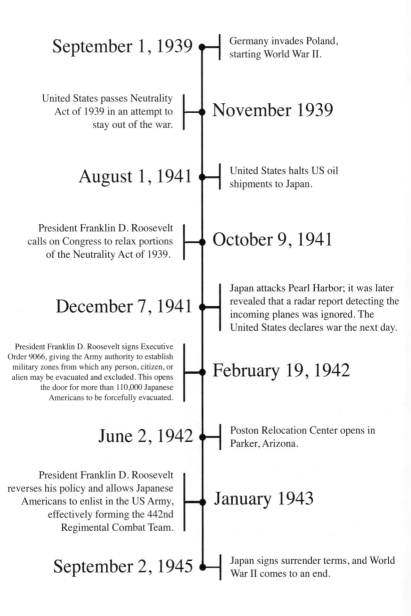

September 1, 1939 — Germany invades Poland, starting World War II.

United States passes Neutrality Act of 1939 in an attempt to stay out of the war. — **November 1939**

August 1, 1941 — United States halts US oil shipments to Japan.

President Franklin D. Roosevelt calls on Congress to relax portions of the Neutrality Act of 1939. — **October 9, 1941**

December 7, 1941 — Japan attacks Pearl Harbor; it was later revealed that a radar report detecting the incoming planes was ignored. The United States declares war the next day.

President Franklin D. Roosevelt signs Executive Order 9066, giving the Army authority to establish military zones from which any person, citizen, or alien may be evacuated and excluded. This opens the door for more than 110,000 Japanese Americans to be forcefully evacuated. — **February 19, 1942**

June 2, 1942 — Poston Relocation Center opens in Parker, Arizona.

President Franklin D. Roosevelt reverses his policy and allows Japanese Americans to enlist in the US Army, effectively forming the 442nd Regimental Combat Team. — **January 1943**

September 2, 1945 — Japan signs surrender terms, and World War II comes to an end.

Confinement Camps in the Southwest, 1942–1946

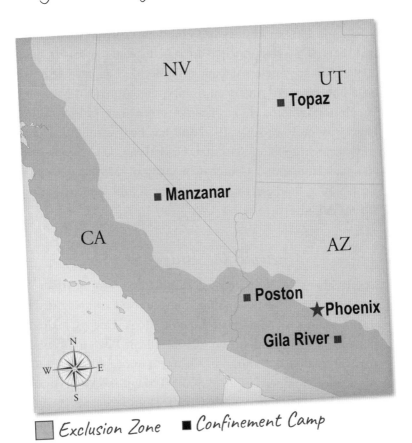

About the Consultant

Stephen Vlastos received his BA from Princeton University (1966) and PhD in History from the University of California, Berkeley (1977). His principal areas of teaching, research, and publication are modern Japanese history; US–Japan relations, including Japanese American history; and American Vietnam War historiography. He has been a professor of history at the University of Iowa since 1976 and has held visiting teaching and research appointments at U.C. Berkeley, U.C. Irvine, the National Humanities Center, University of Michigan Center for Japanese Studies, Tokyo University, Kyoto University, and Doshisha University.

About the Illustrator

Eric Freeberg has illustrated over twenty-five books for children, and has created work for magazines and ad campaigns. He was a winner of the 2010 London Book Fair's Children's Illustration Competition; the 2010 Holbein Prize for Fantasy Art, International Illustration Competition, Japan Illustrators Association; Runner-Up, 2013 SCBWI Magazine Merit Award; Honorable Mention, 2009 SCBWI Don Freeman Portfolio Competition; and 2nd Prize, 2009 Clymer Museum's Annual Illustration Invitational. He was also a winner of the Elizabeth Greenshields Foundation Award.

History is full of storytellers

Take a sneak peek at an excerpt from
Journey to a Promised Land: A Story of the Exodusters
by Allison Lassieur, another story from the
I Am America series.

———————— ◆ ————————

April 5, 1879
Dear Diary,

We had a spelling bee at school today. Me and
Josephine were tied for first at the end. Then
Miss Banneker gave us the hardest word.
Chrysanthemum. I did right terrible with it.
I lost my head after the "R." Jo got it right
though. I'd have been mad if she weren't my best
friend. But it's important that I get my spelling
right if I am to become a teacher. Oh my! I can't
believe I just wrote that down. It's a good thing
Bram can't read yet because I haven't told that
secret to anyone. But it is my deepest desire . . .

Hattie

It was one of those late-spring days when the world is bright and warm, and everything feels possible. Hattie ran the ten crowded blocks from the First Baptist AME Church toward home, her heart pounding hard from excitement or the running, she wasn't sure which. She expertly dodged the dirty pools of water in the street, weaved past the butcher's store that always smelled of blood, and ducked into a narrow alley. It was crisscrossed with a web of clotheslines that dipped heavily with the laundry her mother took in for extra money.

Hattie stopped short, breathing heavily. "Mama!" she called. "I'm home!"

"In the back, baby," came her mother's voice.

Mama was bent over an enormous black iron cauldron, pushing a wooden paddle back and forth in the bubbling, gray water. The familiar scents of wood smoke, lye soap, and steamy clothes hung in the air. She saw Hattie and paused in her work, smiling.

Hattie threw her arms around her mother in a quick hug, feeling those thin, strong arms wrapped around her like a comforting blanket.

"Mama, guess what? Miss Banneker picked me for the recital! I'm going to read a poem in front of everybody!"

Mama beamed with pride. Her rough hand, cracked and hardened through years of work, stroked Hattie's cheek. "Oh, baby, I'm so proud of you," she said.

"Will you come?" Hattie asked, still out of breath from the run. She knew what the answer would be, but she asked anyway, just to hear it.

"I wouldn't miss it for the world," her mother replied. "Papa too. And Abraham, if we can keep him from squirming through the whole thing."

Hattie grinned. She knew how much stock her parents put on learning. When they were enslaved, they hadn't been allowed to learn to read or write. After the Civil War, one of the first things they'd both done was go to school.

"Speaking of your papa, he needs his lunch, and you do too. It's on the table."

Another hug and Hattie dashed through the narrow doorway at the end of the alley. She took the rickety stairs two at a time up to their small two-room apartment. The front room served as kitchen and dining room. The black iron cook stove took up most of the space, along with a table and chairs. The back room held the big, soft bed for

Mama and Papa. Hidden beneath it was the trundle bed for Hattie and Abraham.

Every day when school let out at noon, Hattie came home to take Papa his lunch. Mama always had the food carefully wrapped and waiting. Hattie grabbed the packet and sniffed. Biscuits and sausage, Hattie's favorite.

"Bye, Mama!" she called. But Mama was bent over the tub again, wearily wiping sweat and steam from her forehead.

———————◆———————

Want to read what happens next?

Check out
Journey to a Promised Land:
A Story of the Exodusters